Also by Rodrigo Rey Rosa

THE BEGGAR'S KNIFE
City Lights Books

Dust on Her Tongue

Rodrigo Rey Rosa

*Translated from the Spanish
by Paul Bowles*

CITY LIGHTS BOOKS

San Francisco

Cover design: John Miller, Big Fish Books

Library of Congress Cataloging-in-Publication Data

Rey Rosa, Rodrigo, 1958-
    Dust on her tongue / by Rodrigo Rey Rosa ; translated from the
Spanish by Paul Bowles.
        p.   cm.
    ISBN 0-87286-272-0 : $7.95
    1. Rey Rosa, Rodrigo, 1958-   — Translations into English.
I. Title.
PQ7499.2.R38D8   1992
863 — dc20   92-18152
                                                                CIP

City Lights Books are available to bookstores through our primary
distributor: Subterranean Company. P. O. Box 160, 265 S. 5th St.,
Monroe, OR 97456. 503-847-5274. Toll-free orders 800-274-7826.
FAX 503-847-6018. Our books are also available through library
jobbers and regional distributors. For personal orders and catalogs,
please write to City Lights Books, 261 Columbus Avenue,
San Francisco, CA 94133.
CITY LIGHTS BOOKS are edited by Lawrence Ferlinghetti and
Nancy J. Peters and published at the City Lights Bookstore,
261 Columbus Avenue, San Francisco, CA 94133.

For Jane Tomkiewicz

The action of the tales takes place in Guatemala — not the Guatemala of the news broadcasters, but that of the people whose life continues more or less the same as always, in spite of the violent events that threaten the continuation of that life.

The stories are as compact and severe as theorems, eschewing symbol and metaphor, making their point in terse, undecorated statements which may bewilder the reader unaccustomed to such bareness of presentation.

Paul Bowles

Contents

The Proof

One night while his parents were still on the highway returning from someone's birthday party, Miguel went into the living room and stopped in front of the canary's cage. He lifted up the cloth that covered it, and opened the tiny door. Fearfully, he slipped his hand inside the cage, and then withdrew it doubled into a fist, with the bird's head protruding between his fingers. It allowed itself to be seized almost without resistance, showing the resignation of a person with a chronic illness, thinking perhaps that it was being taken out so the cage could be cleaned and the seeds replenished. But Miguel was staring at it with the eager eyes of one seeking an omen.

All the lights in the house were turned on. Miguel had gone through all the rooms, hesitating at each corner. God can see you no matter where you are, Miguel told himself, but there are not many places suitable for invoking Him. Finally he decided on the cellar because it was dark there. He crouched in a corner under the high vaulted ceiling, as Indians and savages do, face down, his arms wrapped around his legs, and with the canary in his fist between his knees. Raising his eyes into the darkness, which at that moment looked red, he said in a low voice: If you exist, God, bring this bird back to life. As he spoke, he tightened his fist little by little, until his fingers felt the snapping of the fragile bones, and an unaccustomed stillness in the little body.

Then, without meaning to, he remembered María Luisa the maid, who took care of the canary. A little later, when he finally opened his hand, it was as if another, larger hand had been placed on his back — the hand of fear. He realized that the bird would not come back to life. If God did not exist, it was absurd to fear His punishment. The image, the concept of God went out of his mind, leaving a blank. Then, for an instant, Miguel thought of the shape of evil, of Satan, but he did not dare ask anything of him.

He heard the sound of the car going into the garage over his head. Now the fear had to do with this world. His parents had arrived; he heard their voices, heard the car doors slam and the sound of a woman's heels on the stone floor. He laid the inert little body on the floor in the corner, groped in the dark for a loose brick, and set it on top of the bird. Then he heard the chiming of the bell at the front door, and ran upstairs to greet his parents.

All the lights on! exclaimed his mother as he kissed her.

What were you doing down there? his father asked him.

Nothing. I was afraid. The empty house scares me.

His mother went through the house, turning lights off to right and left, secretly astonished by her son's fear.

That night Miguel had his first experience of insomnia. For him not sleeping was a kind of nightmare from which there was no hope of awakening. A static nightmare: the dead bird beneath the brick, and the empty cage.

Hours later Miguel heard the front door open, and the sound of footsteps downstairs. Paralyzed by fear, he fell asleep. María Luisa the maid had finally arrived. It was seven o'clock; the day was still dark. She turned on the kitchen light, set her basket on the table and, as was her custom, removed her sandals in order not to make any noise. She went into the living room and uncovered the canary's cage. The little door was open and the cage was empty. After a moment of panic, during which her eyes remained fixed on the cage hanging in front of her, she glanced around, covered the cage again and returned to the kitchen. Very carefully she took up her sandals and the basket, and went out. When she was no longer in sight of the house she put the sandals on and started to run in the direction of the market, where she hoped to find another canary. It was necessary to replace the one which she thought had escaped due to her carelessness.

Miguel's father awoke at a quarter past seven. He went down to the kitchen, and, surprised to see that María Luisa had not yet come, decided to go to the cellar for the oranges and squeeze them himself. Before going back up to the kitchen, he tried to turn off the light, but his hands and arms were laden with oranges, so that he had to use his shoulder to push the switch. One of the oranges slipped from his arm and rolled across the floor into a corner. He pushed the light on once more. Placing the oranges on a chair, he made a bag out of the front of his bathrobe, dropped them into it, and went to pick up the orange in the corner. And then he noticed the bird's wing sticking out from under the brick. It was not easy for him, but he could guess what had happened. Everyone knows that children are cruel, but how should he react? His wife's footsteps sounded above him in the kitchen. He was ashamed of his son, and at the same time he felt that they were accomplices. He had to hide the shame and the guilt as if they were his own. He picked up the brick, put the bird in his bathrobe pocket, and climbed up to the kitchen. Soon he went on upstairs to his room to wash and dress.

A little later, as he left the house, he met María Luisa returning from the market with the new canary hidden in her basket. She greeted him in an odd fashion, but he did not notice it. He was upset: the hand that he kept in his pocket held the bird in it.

As María Luisa went into the house she heard the voice of Miguel's mother on the floor above. She put the basket on the floor, took out the canary, and ran to slip it into the cage, which she then uncovered with an air of relief and triumph. But then, when she drew back the window curtains and the sun's rays tinted the room pink, she saw with alarm that the bird had one black foot.

It was impossible to awaken Miguel. His mother had to carry him into the bathroom, where she turned on the tap and with her wet hand gave his face a few slaps. Miguel opened his eyes. Then his mother helped him dress and get down the stairs. She seated him at the kitchen table. After he had taken a few swallows of orange juice, he managed to rid himself of his sleepiness. The clock on the wall marked a quarter to eight; shortly María Luisa would be coming in to get him and walk with him to the corner where the school bus stopped. When his mother went out of the room, Miguel jumped down from his chair and ran down into the cellar. Without turning on the light he went to look for the brick in the corner. Then he rushed back to the door and switched on the light. With the blood pounding in his head, he returned to the corner, lifted the brick, and saw that the bird was not there.

María Luisa was waiting for him in the kitchen. He avoided her and ran to the living room. She hurried after him. When on entering the room he saw the cage by the window, with the canary hopping from one perch to the other, he stopped short. He would have gone nearer to make certain, but María Luisa seized his hand and pulled him along to the front door.

On his way to the factory Miguel's father was wondering what he would say to his son when he got home that night. The highway was empty. The weather was unusual: flat clouds like steps barred the sky, and near the horizon there were curtains of fog and light. He lowered the window, and at the moment when the car crossed a bridge over a deep gully he took one hand off the steering wheel and tossed the bird's tiny corpse out.

In the city, while they waited on the corner for the bus, María Luisa listened to the account of the proof Miguel had been granted. The bus appeared in the distance, in miniature at the end of the street. María Luisa smiled. Perhaps that canary isn't what you think it is, she said to Miguel in a mysterious voice. You have to look at it very close. If it has a black foot, it was sent by the Devil. Miguel stared into her eyes, his face tense. She seized him by the shoulders and turned him around.

The bus had arrived; its door was open. Miguel stepped onto the platform. Dirty witch! he shouted.

The driver started up. Miguel ran to the back of the bus and sat down by the window in the last row of seats. There was the squeal of tires, a horn sounded, and Miguel conjured up the image of his father's car.

At the last stop before the school the bus took on a plump boy with narrow eyes. Miguel made a place for him at his side.

How's everything? the boy asked him as he sat down.

The bus ran between the rows of poplars, while Miguel and his friend spoke of the power of God.

Dust on Her Tongue

Another one, she said to herself smiling. She was alone in what she took to be a sordid hotel room. The brick wall did not reach the ceiling, and a gray light came from the next room. She sat up in the sagging bed in which she was unable to sleep. The green pill which she put into her mouth had a bitter flavor, and she made a face as she swallowed it. She had no idea of where she was or of how she had got there. She was lost. But surely this was a hotel. A rooster crowed, and there was the diminishing sound of an automobile's engine in the distance. The bed seemed to move beneath her. Another pill.

In the morning she felt empty, without memory, and with an unpleasant sensation of having consumed too much alcohol. Her feet stuck out at the foot of the bed and her back ached. My god, my god, my god, she murmured, her voice low, ironic and desperate. The floor was of concrete but it was not cold.

She pushed the door, which did not open entirely, and looked at the low gray sky. She was in the patio of a hotel she did not remember having entered. The doors to the rooms bore no numbers. She crossed the courtyard and went out into the street.

She remembered this street, paved with cobblestones. She had seen it the day before, but yesterday was very remote. It seemed to her she remembered the white walls, the tiled roofs. Had there been people in the street? It was a quiet town — too quiet. The silence was not natural, and she knew it boded no good. She did not recall the name of the town.

Why did she see nobody? What day of the week was it? She counted on her fingers. Monday? Sunday? Monday, probably. For a town to be this silent on a Sunday would have upset her too much. The place was dead. She remembered that in the night a rooster had crowed, and that was some consolation, at least. Now she could hear the sound of her own footsteps on the stones. She came to the main square. At the end of the street she saw the side of a church. Something warned her not to go any nearer. She stood still and looked up and down the street. Then she turned and ran back leaving the plaza behind. A cry had come feebly from somewhere. The cry of a child? It had issued from inside the church, or had she imagined it? She ceased running, but continued to walk quickly, and stopped only when she had got inside the hotel. She shut the door, then reopened it to thrust her head out. The street was deserted.

She wanted to ask someone the name of this town. Where was the manager of the hotel?

Ave Maria, she said softly, not daring to call out. She had one hand on her bosom, and walked step by step across the vestibule, looking from side to side.

She remembered a bus filled with people. That was how she had come here. She stopped moving when she got to the gallery. Silence. This was a fourth-class establishment. Why had she spent the night here? She went across the patio to her room and sat down on the bed. She had no watch. Where was the sun? She looked at her hands. What had she done the night before?

A ditty, the words of a song. Yes. A room full of people, pine needles on the floor. A dance? Something she had wanted to forget. A man, the one who had given her the pills. It must be because of him that she was here. She studied the lines in her hand, as though something had been written there. She recalled a dirt road and a river that ran between mountains. It had been getting dark. She remembered that the little bus had jolted and made sudden turnings. But she could not remember getting into it, or what was supposed to be its destination. She did not know whether she had gone towards the north or the south. The memory of the road was rapidly growing dim; she did not want it to disappear, for fear of not finding it again.

She went out into the patio. With this dark sky the sun was invisible, and on the stone floor no object cast a shadow. It seemed as though all the rooms were empty. She heard footsteps from the direction of the street. Frightened, she ran into her room. As she shut the door it occurred to her that whatever was happening out there was something she preferred not to know about. Then she had a flash of recall which could have been the memory of a dream. With a stone in her hand, a heavy stone shaped like an egg, she had pounded the back of a man's head. She had given no warning. The man was her husband.

The sounds coming from the vestibule were men's voices,

one of them high-pitched and shrill. They came across the gallery. There was knocking on the door of the adjoining room on the right. A moment later there came three sharp raps on her own door. She held her breath. The door opened.

Under the bed the air was foul. The sheet hung down from the edge of the bed to the floor, so that she could not see the feet of the person who had come in. She had left the bottle of pills on the bed, and she felt that the man had leaned over and picked it up. She heard him turn on his heels, and the door was shut. Now he knocked on the door of the room on the left.

She looked at the rolls of dust and the ancient spiderwebs which trembled with her breathing. She could not stay under there any longer. As the sound of the feet died away, she felt her fear becoming a sensation of discomfort and shame. Slowly she crawled out from under the bed. She wanted to find the reception clerk and pay her bill. She would go to the main square and get something to eat. Then she would find out when the next bus left for the city. She tried to open the door, but it would not move. She pushed against it with her shoulder; she was locked in.

She did not want to kick the door or call out. She stood on the bed and looked over the top of the dividing wall: the space was too narrow for her body. She sat down. She was hungry and her mouth tasted like paper. She stared fixedly at the floor because she had remembered that before taking the bus she and her husband had been traveling in a plane. The size of the metal wing beneath her window had struck her as absurd. She felt that she had come so far on this trip that she would find it impossible to go back. She stood up and tried the door once more, pushing it with all her strength and kicking it. It was stronger than it looked. She shouted, and had the terrifying conviction that the shout remained in the room. She cried out again.

It was ridiculous! She was sure that it would be useless to complain to the proprietor. She hammered on the door with her fists. Someone had to come.

Overcome by fatigue, she suddenly stretched out on the bed. The wall was damp and smelled musty. Why was she so certain that she was in a hotel? The ceiling was too low. She shut her eyes, wishing that she had someone to massage her neck, which ached. She folded her hands over her abdomen and began to rub her stomach, in order to feel less hungry. She must be calm. It was not easy to lie still, feeling nervous. She had clear memories, but they came from so long ago that she was unable to situate them in time. How old had she been the first time she saw her own face? She recalled the mirror's fancy frame.

Her mother had led her to the room which a few years later was to be hers. The curtains were drawn. Her dead grandmother seemed to be asleep in the bed. Her mother had carried her to the bed, and she had stretched out her hand and touched the nose, already cold. No, said her mother. Give her a kiss. She wondered whether dead people could hear. Now she ceased remembering, and listened for a sound. The light had grown weaker. The frozen face of her grandmother was telling her: You have died, too. You are dead.

Since she had become aware that the door was locked from the outside, since she had screamed and felt that her voice could not be heard, that idea had begun to work in her brain. Now it flashed through her and left her paralyzed. She tried to raise her hand, was unable to, and this gave her a feeling of cold in her breast. The cold descended through her legs to her feet, and returned, as if it were something in her blood. Were her eyes open or shut? She blinked. Now there was no light.

How long had she been there? She could not believe it had been one day. The bed began to rock, and she sprang out of it. Beside herself, she rolled on the floor. She had heard a sound which had now become a roar. The floor also was rocking. She had hit her head. The legs of the bed squeaked.

I have to be dreaming, she told herself. I'm dead and I'm continuing to dream. The idea intrigued her. She imagined that somehow she would be able to follow, step by step, the process of her own decomposition. The flesh would turn into worms; the body would not feel, yet would be conscious. She would be composed of worms. It was the most humble form of transmigration imaginable, but at that moment it was enough. There was a sudden terrible racket. She jumped and fell backwards. She could not possibly be dead, she thought. Bits of earth fell from the ceiling. Were they burying her? I'm alive! she cried. And she repeated under her breath: I'm alive. There was dust on her tongue. She wanted to spit.

A few moments of calm. She did not want to open her eyes, but neither did she want to keep them shut. She began to feel sleepy, knowing that she should not fall asleep. It seemed to her that if she slept she would forget who she was, and that when she awoke she would have been changed into someone else: the tutelary goddess of a colony of worms. Madness. Finally she was overcome by sleep.

She came to. Two men were dragging her across the patio in a not too uncomfortable posture. She realized that she was not afraid of them. The warmth of their arms was reassuring: she was cold.

They went out into the street. The sky was red. She felt that she did not need the two men in order to walk, but she allowed them to go on supporting her. From time to time the earth trembled and there was that muffled roar that she had heard earlier. They went through a low door into a circular enclosure. The cloth walls moved in the wind. The men were young. One of them set to rubbing her arms and legs. Then he made her open her mouth so he could look inside.

Does your head ache?

Where am I? she said. What happened?

You may have a fractured skull, señora, although I don't think so. Try to be calm. I'll do what I can.

But I don't remember anything, she protested. Don't you understand?

Yes, I understand, he said. You'll remember.

From the center of the ceiling hung a wire basket. There, among other objects which she recognized as hers, she saw the bottle of pills; it was the proof of an infraction she did not remember having committed. The owner of the hotel arrived to present her bill.

In the afternoon they told her that she would leave for the city, where her husband expected her. A rented car arrived to pick her up. They crossed the partially destroyed town. Men wearing green uniforms were beginning to clear away the rubble. The cornfields were ruined and the earth was the color of ashes. Beside the road, on a treeless hill, a kneeling Indian was burning incense. He swung the burner and the smoke dissolved in the gray air.

Privacy

At one time I dreamed of becoming a saint; I am not a sage, nor am I even reasonable. Recounting this is a kind of punishment.

I scarcely slept the night before, and if I slept, it was like being at the bottom of a well. I saw — either asleep or awake; I don't know which — the shoulders of a very tall woman, and rain over a river. Toward dawn I thought: I'm not as I ought to have been.

I got up the same as always, washed, and dressed with care. I can't forget the way the hotel mirror made my face look; I shaved badly, almost without glancing at myself, and then I hid the razor up my sleeve. I went out into the street and opened my umbrella. I remember thinking that the repeated sounds made by the light rain falling on the stretched black cloth were affecting my state of mind. When I arrived at the address they had given me, I asked someone for the time. I let a few minutes go by before I went in.

When one has reached the point I have reached, any act can be different from what it appears to be: cutting one's nails, going through a doorway.

On the other side there was a neglected garden. Three workmen were pulling on a rope attached to the top of a tree which was about to fall over. At the end of the garden, facing eastwards there was a row of red-colored buildings, like abandoned temples. The last one in the line was different from the others: its facade had no pillars, and it was built almost entirely of glass. I went in there, and a heavily made-up woman approached me.

"Where is the reception desk?" I asked her.

"What reception desk?"

"The office."

"Which office?"

"Who's in charge?" I said. "Doesn't anyone work here?"

"Yes, yes. The doctors. Come."

She went ahead of me; we crossed a sky-blue and yellow corridor with many doors along the walls. It was as if the last particle of life had been removed from the air. The woman opened a door on the right and waved me in. She smiled from the corridor, shaking her head, and then she shut the door.

The room had no windows; a feeble light came in through a slit in the ceiling. I looked at my shoes, and had the sensation of not knowing who I was. I lifted my heels slightly, raised my eyes and looked at the door handle. Slowly the door moved inward. I crossed my legs.

The doctor leaned partially into the room, turning to say back over his shoulder: "They ought not to laugh." Then he greeted me. The dialogue was brief. I asked after my sister, and he told me she was doing well. "Astonishingly well" was what he said. But he wanted us to talk about me. "Would you like something to drink?" he asked me, pointing to the refrigerator in the corner. Somewhat confused, I said yes. It disturbed me that I should not have noticed the object until he called my attention to it. The drink tasted of mint. "You write, don't you?" he said, and without ceasing to look at me he took out a sheet of paper and laid it on the table. He was about to put his hand into his breast pocket. "I have a pen," I told him. "What do you want me to write?"

"Whatever you like. But fill the page, see?"

"Who's going to read it?" I said. I was annoyed.

"Don't worry. I, and one or two of my colleagues. The more we know about you people the better."

I did not feel like replying. As he got up to go out, he touched my shoulder. I stood up. On one of the floor tiles there was an ink stain. From my sleeve I took a sheet of carbon paper and another blank sheet, put them under the paper he had given me, and sat down to write.

I had scarcely filled the page and hidden the sheet of carbon and the copy when the doctor opened the door. "Ready?" he said. "Ready," I told him, smiling. Without glancing at it, he put the paper into a black portfolio. "Wonderful," he said absently. "Follow me."

We went out and turned to the right. The hallway was very long and it occurred to me that it must form a connection between the backs of the other buildings. A nurse came up to us, and the doctor handed her the portfolio. She smiled and walked on. I was beginning to feel tired, and I had the impression that we were climbing. The doctor walked two or three paces ahead of me. The shadow of my head skipped between his feet. I felt inexplicably sad.

I stopped. Here the doors were numbered. There was a small arched window at the end of the hallway. The tops of some lead-colored trees moved in the wind behind the streams of rain. "Have we been climbing?" I inquired. He took my arm and opened a door. "Go in." He reached in and turned on the light. This room was no different from the other, save that in one corner there was a cot. The rain hit a window in the far wall.

It seems useless to relate what happened afterward; perhaps it would be wiser to stop. On the inner side of the window I saw a crevice of light, like the flame of an invisible thread as it burns. I took a step, and the light did not move. I was tense. I reached into my sleeve and threw myself at the window.

When I came to I was sitting on the cot, leaning against the wall. My eyes were tired of looking at the ceiling. I lowered my head and saw a dark grayish oval-shaped stain on the sheet between my legs. The nurse finally came in. "And the doctor?" I asked her. She looked vague. "I don't know what can have happened," she began. I gave vent to a guffaw for which I make no excuse. "Forget about it," I said. "He's dead."

My clothing hung on the back of a chair. When the woman went out I stood up and pulled out the carbon paper and the copy which I had hidden in my shirt. Everything is different, I said to myself. I'm another man. There was a strange glow around my hands, on the floor, throughout the room.

The Burial

The city has grown, thought Antonio Blanch, viewing it from above, as the plane banked and curved in a cloudless sky. Returning to his birthplace after several years' absence was like catching up the thread of a tale only partially read. A few months earlier a voluminous correspondence had sprung up between him and his grandfather, in which the old man, giving strange reasons, had persuaded him to return.

The plane's wheels touched the ground; the runway was full of potholes. The airport had not changed. As he waited to get through customs, he was hoping that no one had come to pick him up; he would have enjoyed putting up at some hotel in the middle of the city and spending a few days by himself, in order to see the city through the eyes of an outsider. With his luggage examined and his passport stamped, he went toward the exit and pushed against the heavy door. He saw no one he knew. In the street also he saw only strangers. As he was about to get into a taxi his mother's voice stopped him. The driver took out the suitcase, which was already in the trunk, and Antonio walked toward the car where his father sat. I didn't think anyone would be coming, he told them.

On the drive to the house, they said that everything in the country was going from bad to worse. It was true that the city had grown larger; perhaps from the air he had not been able to see that the growth was an illness, but it was a fact that most of the new dwellings were of plywood. His father wanted to sell the warehouse and move to a safer place, but there was no buyer. His mother's father, with whom he had been corresponding, had just moved in with them. He was in good health considering his age, but he needed constant attention. For the time being, she said, he and his grandfather would be sharing a room.

The following day, as they walked in the park, the old man spoke with him. Almost word for word he repeated what he had said in his letters. His voice was low and calm, and his eyes shone. He wanted to spend the end of his life in the solitude of a cave, like the saints in the wilderness, where he could await death in silence, and alone. But he was afraid he would not be allowed to do such a thing. Then, not without having first assured himself that he could count on Antonio's discretion, he asked him to take him to a nearby old-people's home that very afternoon, when Antonio's parents would be away from the house.

Señor Blanch heard the news with anger. After all, he said to himself, the old man was free to choose. If it did not suit him to live in the house with them, it was not their fault.

Antonio ate his soup in silence. His grandfather had asked him to let a day go by before telling anyone the name of the place where he had gone, but his mother's pleas were becoming hysterical.

Calm yourself, her husband told her.

She rose from the table and left the room.

The next morning Antonio took his mother to see the old man. She felt better after speaking with him; he seemed content and in a good mood. Here he could talk all he wanted without boring anyone, and it was a consolation, if perhaps an empty one, to be able to compare himself with other men of his age, and to realize that he was not at all in a poor condition.

They walked around the small garden, and a little before evening said goodbye.

I'd be so happy if you'd come back to the house, she told him from the doorway.

The old man smiled. Yes, yes. This isn't a prison.

A week went by. Now Antonio had to persuade his parents to take a vacation. I think Papa needs it, he said to his mother. Besides, it might be easier to bring Grandfather back home if you're not here.

It was summer and the heat was growing more intense, so that it was not too difficult to get his father to agree to close his office for a few days.

Antonio was right, said Señor Blanch, screwing the cap onto a bottle of suntan lotion.

These days of rest beside the sea — the sun, the sand, the sound of the waves, the evening walks along the port, the music of guitars and drums — these things helped to mitigate the domestic worries. On this island, removed from time, Señora Blanch came to regard the unexpected behavior of her father as a good sign. It was a manifestation of vitality and firmness, a protection against old age.

Ten days later they were back in the city, only to find that the dread they had kept at bay during the short interval had after all been justified. In the midst of the crowd at the airport, as he greeted his mother, Antonio whispered in her ear that her father was dead.

Dispirited, they silently piled the luggage into the trunk. The funeral is this afternoon, Antonio said. His mother burst into tears, and her husband helped her into the car. He died at home, Antonio told them, seating himself at the wheel, I was with him.

There were not many people in the church. The coffin, black and decorated, seemed to filter the dark; the four candles burned without giving light. The deep, mellow voice of the priest floated in the nave like a cloud: I created the light and the darkness, says the word of the Lord. And thus we say that he who destroys the eye makes blind, and that he who can save the life of another and fails to do so, has killed him. But God takes our life in order to give us another life.

Antonio was thinking of the physical world. Where might his grandfather be? In his mind's eye he saw a great space whose light and darkness came together without blending, like wine and oil. He breathed the incense, felt the weight of his body, heard the creaking of his black shoes. His father turned his head to look at him, gravely opening and closing his eyes. His mother looked straight ahead, beyond the priest, beyond the high crucifix, and possibly beyond the wall of the church.

De profundis clamavi, chanted the choir. Antonio, together with his father, an old friend of his grandfather, and a distant relative, lifted the heavy coffin.

The funeral procession moved down the muddy street. Through the car window Antonio's mother looked at the faces without seeing them, was aware of voices without hearing them. Her grief, combined with the slow pace, made the place seem like a different city.

They lowered the coffin, the earth fell onto it. A young workman counted the bricks while another mixed sand, cement and water. They sealed the tomb.

Far from there, in a spacious cave, was the grandfather. A fire blazed near the wall, and on the damp stone his shadow was a bird; then it changed into a wolf, a lizard (now the old man was crouching). As the fire died out, the shadow became a huge dark egg.

Still Water

On the silt and pebble-covered floor of the lagoon lay the body of a man. His open eyes seemed to be looking at the sun of a lower, liquid sky. A small black and yellow fish swam along the ridge of his leg, another nibbled at his ear. He had been down there for some time, and his unmoving body had become a part of the watery landscape. His face seemed peaceful, but now and then it was as though his lips curled in an expression of disgust. The seaweed moved with his hair in the gentle current. As long as the mud adhered to it, his body changed slowly; the eyes, which originally had been hollow, pushed out of the swollen face. They had lost their color; they would have seen only blackness. The belly grew to be enormous, and one night the body rose up out of the black mud, the muck covered all trace of where it had lain, and the flesh came into the open as it was propelled by the waves to the shore.

The police commissioner of Flores leaned over the body, his handkerchief pressed to his nose. There were few things which displeased him as much as an unexplained death; his bloodshot eyes slowly searched for some sign of violence. He only found the marks left by the hands of the fishermen who had discovered the corpse and pulled it out of the water, and the fish-bitten face and clenched hands. The commissioner had someone force the fists open: one was empty and the other held a bit of earth and a stone. From its size he judged the body to be that of a foreigner. He raised his head and folded his handkerchief.

Richard Ward, an American, had come to the Petén nine months earlier, and had purchased a piece of land facing the lagoon of Itzá, where he built a small cottage. He intended to retire there with his wife Lucy, who was waiting in Wisconsin for news of him. Two weeks before the body was found, Richard Ward had been seen in a shop in Flores, and then he had disappeared. His servant Rafael Colina was taken to the police station, where he was questioned. No result came of this, nor of the search made of his hut, on Ward's land. They kept him for a few hours, and after administering the customary beating, let him go.

Lucy Ward arrived in Flores one wet Sunday in September. She was stout, with graceful arms and legs. At the police station they gave her the little box containing the ashes: 37, she read on the cover, *Sr. R. Ward*. A police car took her to the property, where Rafael was expecting her.

She wandered around the terrain, examining the landscape with the questioning expression of someone looking at an abstract painting he fails to understand; then she realized with some surprise that it pleased her. She went into the cottage, looked around, and decided to spend the night there. Later, on her way to sleep, she thought of her husband, and was grateful to him for having found this place. She decided to try living there for a while.

From the outset it was as though the absence of human companionship, an absence which she had dreaded, was compensated for by the feverish life of the plants, the activity of the insects, and the tenuous presence of Rafael. Little by little she became aware of the forest's tiny miracles, and she learned how to resign herself to the inconveniences: the ever-present ants, the constant sweating, the mosquitoes at twilight and at dawn.

After supper she would go out and sit in the rocking chair and stay listening to the voices of the earth, metallic and hypnotic. During the day she liked to walk among the trees along a narrow path cleared by her husband. She would walk until she was tired, and relax among the vines to breathe in the scent of branches and dead leaves. From time to time she caught a strange butterfly, or gathered flowers whose names she did not know.

One night when rain fell unceasingly, the sound of it on the palm-thatched roof kept her from sleeping and for the first time she was troubled by her husband's death. Like the rain that was starting to drip into the room, fear began to seep into her consciousness. A heavy drop landed next to her pillow; she got up and pushed the bed into the middle of the room. There were flashes of lightning. As she was finally on her way to falling asleep, by a bolt of lightning she saw Rafael in the doorway, watching her. She blinked her eyes, and considered stretching her arm out to light a match; then she realized with relief that she had been wrong. The face was a stain in the wood. She breathed deeply and sank into sleep.

In the morning when the sun was high, she opened her eyes and heard Rafael working in the kitchen. The air was sweet with the smell of corn. Needles of sunlight pushed between the slits in the ceiling, a fly buzzed. She made her bed and dressed to go out.

Morning, said Rafael, showing his yellow teeth.

She went to sit on the porch. Rafael put the tray on the small table beside her chair. As he was pouring her coffee, she turned and looked into the distance, saying in a hushed voice: I've been thinking of Don Ricardo.

He stared at her an instant, surprised; then he looked away and lifted his head. Don Ricardo, he said. The light moved on the surface of the lagoon. Lucy raised her cup, and he turned and went into the kitchen.

That morning, instead of taking her walk in the forest, Lucy went to the end of the dock and spread out a towel to sunbathe. She thought of the past; it was empty and vague. Memory dissolved in the heat.

The sun burned her face. She heard Rafael push his rowboat into the water. Sitting up, she saw him row past the dock.

I'm going to see if there's any fish, he told her, continuing to row toward the other bank.

She lay face down, looking at the white flowers under the water; then she shut her eyes in order not to think.

The heat became intense. She plunged into the water and swam back and forth at the end of the dock. Then she came out and let the sun dry her. On her way to the house, she noticed that the door to the hut under the banana plants was open. She glanced behind her — only the still water — and walked rapidly to the door, peering into the dark interior.

There was a large earthenware pot in the corner, resting on some stones that kept it from touching the floor; underneath it were ashes and dead embers. She stopped, astounded, in the middle of the room. In the air, near her face, an enormous toad was staring at her. It opened its mouth, and she saw the glass jar and the cord that suspended it from above. The toad moved, pushing its four toes against the glass. Her fear was transformed into pity. She touched the jar with a fingernail, and the toad raised and lowered its eyelids. The cover had been pierced with a nail. In the bottom of the jar were some blades of grass and a fly. She turned it around and held it close to her face so she could examine the toad's skin.

From some distance away came a hollow wooden sound. From the doorway she saw the boat in the middle of the lagoon. Rafael was rowing in a standing position, a stroke on the left, then on the right, never taking his eyes off the shore. She felt a trickle down her spine, and she realized that her hair was dripping wet. She went out of the hut, leaving drops of water on the floor where she had stood.

That noon Rafael served her a fish stew. She tasted it without pleasure, and left it almost intact. He asked her if anything was the matter with the food. No, the food was good, but the sun had taken away her appetite. After he had disappeared into his hut to take his siesta, she went to the kitchen and prepared herself a dish of fruit.

She must speak to Rafael. His treatment of the toad was cruel. She thought of the wrinkled skin, the unhappy eyes behind the glass. Sitting on the porch, she looked out over the lagoon and thought of her husband's ashes.

She rose from the rocking chair and went silently — the

afternoon was very still — to the open door of the hut.

Rafael, crouching with his back to her, was playing with the toad, which he had taken out of the jar and was poking with a stick. The cornered toad puffed itself out threateningly; above its eyes had appeared pointed black ridges, like horns.

She took a few steps back, and called out loudly: Rafael! He jumped up and stuck his head outside the door.

I'm sorry, she said. I need some lemons. Do you think you could go and buy some?

When Rafael had gone, taking the road to the village, Lucy drew back the bolt and pushed open the door to the hut. The toad was once again in the jar. She unscrewed the top, put the jar on the floor, and urged the toad out of the room with her foot. She bolted the door again and went back to the porch. The sun was getting close to the horizon.

Rafael returned at dusk. There were no lemons, he said as he walked past her, on his way to the hut. Lucy watched him as she rocked in the chair. She saw him open the door and go in. Then suddenly he rushed out again, as if he had been pushed. He looked here and there on the ground, behind the bushes that surrounded the hut, under the banana plants, in the ditch beside the path, and between the stalks of the canebrake. He returned to the hut and searched once more, and after that he stood in the doorway looking out.

What is it? Lucy called. She saw him coming toward her, his head lowered.

Is something wrong?

Somebody went into my house.

The mosquitoes were biting her. Somebody? When?

Rafael glanced behind him. You didn't see anybody?

There was a full moon, and the air was still. Before supper,

Lucy went out and stood on the shore looking at the sky. She knew that her lie had offended Rafael. For a moment she felt like admitting her wrongdoing, but then silence seemed the better course.

The food was on the table. Listlessly she finished all the fish; this was to please him. (Now she felt sorry for him.) In a low voice she begged his pardon. Rafael served himself and said good night. When the candle in his hut no longer burned, she went into her room.

In the night she awoke to feel a weight on her abdomen. She felt it move upward across her chest. It was something cold, it was crawling now on her neck, and it stopped at her mouth. She could not move: her limbs were heavy. Then she saw the toad, its body swelling . . .

She threw back the sheet and jumped out of bed. There was a bitter taste in her mouth. She seized a flashlight, ran into the bathroom, and tried to be sick. Letting the water run, she put her head under the tap. Then she sat down on the bathmat and found that she was unable to get up again. In the mirror she saw the flashlight shining.

Coralia

"She's a great woman," the man said. He was seated at a table next to the counter in a small restaurant. "When we leave here I'll take you to her house. You'll love her."

He was speaking with a woman who was, apparently, a foreigner with auburn hair and a very white face. The man wore a light blue sportshirt. He had gray hair and a suntan.

At the next table two young people were listening to the conversation while they waited to be served. "He's talking about her," the young man said with a smile. Before going into the restaurant they had been speaking of Coralia. "She has an ego as big as a cathedral," he had declared as a kind of summation before pushing the door open. "But since you're going to be here it would be worthwhile knowing her."

"She sounds interesting," the girl said, peering at the crumpled sheet of paper that served as a menu.

He had ordered a fish from the lake, and he almost choked on a bone when the woman named Coralia appeared in the doorway. She crossed the room between the tables, her head held high, glancing neither right nor left, until she came to the counter.

"She's a little near-sighted," the young man murmured into his companion's ear.

The gray-haired man had risen to greet her.

"Señor Méndez! What luck!" she said. "I've been looking for you. I tried to call you, but my telephone's dead. I thought I'd make the call from here. And here I find you."

"Here I am, at your service, señora. What can I do for you?"

"Imagine," began Coralia, sitting down in the chair that Señor Méndez had drawn up to the table. "Ricardito — he's my son" — she explained for the benefit of the auburn-haired woman, "had to take the station wagon to the city, and I've got to go to the other side of the river for a load of wood. I wanted to ask you if I might rent your truck."

"Certainly not." Señor Méndez rejected the idea with his whole body. "I'd be delighted to go and fetch the wood myself. Right now, if you like. Where is it? What an idea!" He looked at the auburn-haired woman. "Rent her my truck, indeed!"

Coralia stood up.

"You don't know how grateful I am. The wood is at Domingo's. It's already paid for. It's stacked beside the shop there. Do you want me to go with you? Or shall I wait for you at home and we'll have coffee? She must come too, of course."

As she turned to go out, Coralia caught sight of the two young people at the other table.

"Enrique!" she cried.

The young man was wiping his lips.

"I can't believe it," Coralia told him. "How long have you been here? Why haven't you been by to see me?"

"We just got here," he told her. He stood up, kissed her cheek, and hugged her.

"See you shortly," said Señor Méndez on his way to the door. "We'll be there at five for that coffee."

Coralia watched him go, an expression of approval on her face.

"You haven't changed," Enrique told her. "You can still get people to do things for you. Who's the gentleman?"

"Señor Méndez is an angel. The *finca* called El Rosario is his. A man of the old school, a bit hard on his peons, but a good friend."

"Coralia, Rita." Enrique presented the girl, who had been watching the other woman with interest.

Coralia sighed deeply.

"Enrique," she said. "Tell me. What have you been doing with your life? I don't even know where you've been living."

He had just paid the check. Exhaling noisily, he said: "What a meal! Shall we go?"

Outside, a car shone in the sunlight. The girl skipped down the steps and went to sit on the bumper.

"It's three o'clock," Enrique told Coralia. "We've got time to take a drive. We'll take you home afterward."

Coralia glanced at the asphalt road that led to her house. "I'd do anything rather than go on foot in this sun," she admitted.

The back seat was piled with suitcases. Coralia, sitting in front between Enrique and the girl, suggested that they take the Jaibal road.

"They just recently opened it up as far as the ridge," she said.

"There's a wonderful view of the whole lake."

Enrique turned the car around and speeded up once they were on the highway.

After a long silence while the car climbed up the side of a mountain, Coralia began to talk. She was sitting with her legs crossed under her, and she seemed to be watching something that moved with the car at a height of several feet above the road.

Her life at present, aside from the inconveniences attendant upon living in a village, was marvelous. She informed them that she was a very candid person, and that she liked to tell the whole story from the beginning. She kept nothing back (she did not know what shame was) and that whoever objected to this should say so at the start. Seeing that Rita seemed interested, she decided to speak of her past. Enrique already knew the story, but he claimed to be eager to hear a new recounting of it.

The dirt road they had turned off onto passed through coffee plantations and after making a steep descent came to an end at the foot of a high ridge. They got out and climbed along a path to the summit, where a cool breeze was blowing. The three sat down on the grass, facing the lake. Already in Rita's eyes Coralia was an extraordinary being. She had heard how she had emerged victorious from a hard childhood, with a drunken father who persecuted her and a mother who was vain and indifferent. Very early in life she had learned that escape was possible by creating an interior life. She spoke of a spiral staircase in a convent where she had been a student. She had only recently arrived there, and at bedtime, as she started up the stairs, she had fainted. It was then that she heard a voice — a man's voice — which told her that no one could harm her. Each time she tried to climb those stairs the same thing happened. The nuns had finally given her a tiny room on the lower floor. Nevertheless, every time she had the opportunity she slipped off to the staircase. Even though she was afraid of fainting, she liked to hear the voice.

She had learned to sing at the convent. They put her into the choir, and she was at her happiest during the hours they passed chanting in the chapel. Now and then she considered becoming a nun, attracted by the Mother Superior, who often spoke to them of the joys of marriage and the embrace of the Savior.

No one came to visit her except an aunt and an uncle. Each week they brought something for her: sometimes sweets and often, when the nuns were not looking, books. This was how Coralia had come to study oriental beliefs. She read everything, and although she did not understand what the beliefs were about, the experience of reading seemed to her like sinking into the waters of wisdom.

At that time her splendid hair hung down to her waist. The nuns had wanted to have it cut, for fear of parasites. But fortunately someone had intervened, and she was allowed to remain with it, on condition that she keep it always absolutely clean. But it was torture to be obliged to comb the snarls out of it every morning and night, and finally she had rebelled. It was ridiculous that they should not let her do as she wished with her own hair!

One day in class a nun noticed that she was scratching her head. She pulled her out into the corridor and carried out an investigation. "Lice!" she cried, and dragged her to the Mother Superior's office. It took three nuns to hold her while a fourth rapidly cut the tresses with a pair of shears.

That afternoon she wrote to her mother, asking to be taken

out of the convent. The woman replied that she was sorry, but the thing was impossible, as she was completely preoccupied with her divorce proceedings. Coralia determined that never again would she speak to her. That Sunday her uncle came to visit, and upon learning what had happened, offered to help her.

For a moment Coralia was quiet; she was thinking of the man's goodness. She was about to continue, when Enrique pointed to the red sun, already touching the rims of the mountains.

"It's after five," he remarked, glancing at his wristwatch.

"Poor Señor Méndez." Rita had stood up.

Coralia seemed surprised by the interruption.

"Really, Rita," she was saying as they went down the path, "life is wonderful." Rita looked back at her over her shoulder and smiled. "But what is really wonderful is to be in love."

Enrique was already in the car.

"Have you been in love?" Coralia asked her when they had started up. Before the girl could reply she continued: "One falls in love only once, maybe twice. It happened to me twice. The first time was more powerful. It went on for ten years. The second . . ."

In the uncomfortable silence which followed, Enrique spoke.

"Is Señor Méndez a patient man?"

"The second time," Coralia went on, glancing at Rita out of the corner of her eye, and pointing at Enrique, "I fell in love with him."

It seemed as though the girl had not heard her, for in her face as she looked out at the trees illumined by the headlights at the side of the road, her expression did not change.

"Has he told you about it?" Coralia wanted to know, but Rita did not answer.

"Have you told her?"

Enrique laughed.

"I haven't told her anything."

A few yards after he had crossed the river Enrique had to make way suddenly for a small truck with blinding headlights which bore down upon them from the other direction.

Rita turned to look. "Señor Méndez!" she exclaimed.

Señor Méndez had stopped his truck at the edge of the river.

They saw him climb into the back of the truck and, leaning against the cabin's partition, kick the logs furiously out of the truck, so that they rolled down the bank into the water and floated off downstream. The sky was full of stars.

The Truth

The rain had stopped and the sunlight, tempered by the translucent curtains, shone into the spacious dining room. A man, seated at the head of the table, a woman, and three small girls were eating their dessert in silence. It was a heavy silence. To the father's right, there was an empty chair, a half-eaten pastry.

"You're a liar," the father had said. The son had glanced up at him without saying anything. Black hairs stuck out of the man's nostrils. He looked at the child almost scornfully. Not allowing himself to cry, the boy had left the table and gone to his room. He lay down on the bed and opened a book, hoping to lose himself in its pages.

Somewhat later he stood up and looked into the mirror. For some time now his face had begun to please him. His lips, which had always struck him as being too thick, now seemed

to suggest an expression of strength and humor. He had brown
eyes that, half shut under the dark brows, were like those of a
man. He combed his hair and stepped out into the corridor.
Softly he went down the stairs and into the garden, using the
back door.

The stable was only a short distance from the house, a building of concrete blocks with a tin roof. The light entered
obliquely through a skylight, skeins of garlic were hung here
and there to keep out the bats, and the air smelled of bran and
urine. One of the horses snorted when he became aware of the
boy. He went into the stall of a black mare and saddled her.

Once in the saddle he ceased being his father's son, to
become a warrior. He trotted out along the dirt lane, and rode
toward the mountains that surrounded the city. Barefoot children, washerwomen, beggars and drunks watched him go by
— envy, hatred, desire, admiration. Soon the huts had been left
behind, and he began to climb a path among the trees. The far-
off noise of traffic on the highway was a hostile sound. It was
the road of the white man. The red sun went behind the
clouds. When he got to the top he pulled on the reins and
stood up in the stirrups to look around him. Then he went at a
gallop toward the gap crossed by the ancient aqueduct, for
from there he could, without being seen, watch the winding
highway below.

He hitched the mare where he always left her when he came
up here, hidden behind some evergreen oaks, and went down
the hill to the footwalk. In the middle of the bridge he stopped
and leaned over. There were stones missing from the wall here,
and through a crack he could see the army of cars which the
city spewed out each afternoon. The old stones were danger-
ously loose. A few days ago the idea had occurred to him, the

idea of letting a stone fall, and, like a god from on high, changing the life of a mortal.

"Why did you do it?" the owner of the long black car chosen by the rock, would ask him. "Why?" He would try to break free of the chauffeur's grip. At last, giving up, he would say: "If you'll allow me, sir, perhaps I can explain."

"I've been coming to this part of the bridge for some time, to watch the cars go by. It's something worth seeing, if you manage to forget everything else, forget yourself and the bridge and the road, so that there is nothing but the stream of lights, the two streams, one red and one white. The other evening I was thinking: God knows who might not be going by underneath me at this minute — a murderer, or a saint. Someone with the key to the puzzle of my life, or of my ruin. But, sir, who are you? Why did my stone land on your car?"

The rock he was leaning on was covered with moss. It moved slightly. He scratched off the moss with a fingernail: the stone was porous. It was beginning to get dark, and the drivers of the cars had turned on their lights. What would happen if the car that was hit by the stone were driven by a woman? The car would be red; he did not manage to picture the woman. His fingernail was black, and the rock had no moss on it. Perhaps an evil angel was lurking nearby, because he thought: Push it. Now. But the voice he heard was his own.

He pushed the rock.

There was a squeal of brakes, and then the noise of cars colliding — two, three, four. For a moment there was silence. He jumped up and began to run, bent over, hidden by the parapet. When he got to the end of the aqueduct he looked down. From the chaos in the middle of the road, a man raised his hand and pointed to where he stood.

"Hey there!" he shouted.

He jumped down to the path and went on running. The men were yelling; two of them began to climb the cliff behind him. He was running and slipping; the shouts were missiles being shot at his back. If he succeeded in reaching the oak grove before the men got to the level of the bridge, he would be safe. It struck him as strange that while he was bending all his efforts to avoid the roots and holes in the path, he was thinking that he would rather not have been alone, that it would have been good to have someone with whom he could discuss it afterward. He stumbled and rolled on the ground. He could not see the men, but their voices sounded near. He got to the grove and stopped to catch his breath. It was dark here among the trees. He came to the mare, and was starting to unhitch her, when a voice, that of a boy, made him turn.

"I saw you," it told him.

He looked at the other as if he did not understand.

"I saw you throw the stone." It was the voice of blackmail.

The mare's mane was twisted; a fly lit on her ear; she flicked it away. The reflection in her black eye gave him the answer. He and the other boy both wore white shirts.

"You saw me," he said, letting go of the reins. They were the same size; he was wearing boots and his enemy was barefoot. He lowered his head. His father's words were being borne out. The mare champed at the bit, and he jumped upon the other, who fell on his back on the ground. He sat astride him and said between his teeth:

"You didn't see me. I saw you."

He punched the other in the mouth, and squeezed his knees together more tightly. The boy squirmed.

When the two men arrived, out of breath, he stood up.

"I saw him," he said, pointing. "I saw him push the stone."

The boy spat blood and raised his hands to his mouth. One of the men, whose forehead was bleeding, seized the boy by his shirt and kicked him.

"Get up," he told him. "We'll see if you've killed my wife, you whelp."

The boy was crying. He tried to defend himself, but it was hard for him to speak with his mouth full of blood. He had not said three words before the man hit him. The mare lifted a leg and set it down. Her master put his foot in the stirrup.

"What's your name?" the other man asked, when he was astride her.

He told him. His voice had an uncomfortable ring to it. He hastened to add:

"I'm sorry about your wife."

The two men, with the barefoot boy, went out of the grove.

He turned the mare around and started ahead slowly because the path was narrow and there was no light.

Even though he told himself that there was nothing to fear, and that his word was worth more than that of the other, his legs trembled and he was worried. "There was no other way," he thought, and on the other hand: "You're a liar," his father insisted.

It was a good thing that it was night, and that the mare was black, and that in the world of men nothing was certain. From a curve in the path he caught a glimpse of the city with its lights; it was as though he had returned from somewhere far away. The jaunt had almost come to an end. Smoke rose from the huts, and the mare hastened her step.

When he dismounted he felt vulnerable. He took a handful of salt from a pail and gave it to the mare: he liked to feel her rough tongue on his palm. He patted her neck and chest, and ran toward the house.

Dinner was on the table. Everyone seemed to be in a good humor.

"How far did you go?" his mother asked him.

"Not very far," he said. He looked at his sisters and began to cut his meat. He did not want to be asked any more questions.

No one would believe him if he told what had happened. He would have liked to discuss it with someone, but it was good too to have a secret. It made him feel like laughing to think that his secret was impenetrable, that not even he would be able to betray it.

His father was staring at him.

"Look at your hands," he said.

The black fingernail stood out against the white tablecloth.

"What were you doing?"

He raised his hand as if he wanted to see it in a stronger light. Turning toward his father, he thought: "I'm not a liar," and he realized that he was going to tell him the truth.

"I'm not sure," he said. "I think I killed a woman."

His sisters laughed.

"It's not a joke," he said. "I let a stone fall off the bridge, and she was underneath."

"Swear it's the truth," said his youngest sister.

"I swear."

"Why do you enjoy telling lies?" asked his father.

He wiped his lips and looked at the napkin. He did not intend to answer. Folding his arms, he sat back in his chair.

His mother passed him the bowl of fruit.

"What are you thinking about?" she asked him.

He imagined the other, who was paying for him: a damp cell, the dark.

"Nothing," he answered.

There was a short silence. Then they finished eating their supper.

Angelica

Memories had begun to fill Angelica Pierri's mind. All morning long she had seemed removed from everything. Her world had suddenly been transformed; death had touched her from within.

Since the telephone call she had felt weak. Although several times she had insisted to herself that it was true, she could not bring herself to believe what they had told her. Eventually she understood that the dead do not go away, but remain inside those whom they leave behind. With him who had died she felt the shame brought by death when it is caused by human hands.

Halfway between dreaming and daydreaming she saw herself and Manuel from a distance. The rhythm of her breathing, the colors in the room, the sounds coming from outside, all seemed to belong to the past. It was as though she could not reach the present moment; she had taken refuge in the deepest part of her being, and the future did not exist.

The smoke of the cigarette hurt her eyes. She blinked, put the filter between her lips. It would have been good to believe that she had already lived this moment, that her entire life had been lived through uncounted times, that it would be repeated once again. In the oblique morning light the particles of dust floated in slow circles, the smoke of the cigarette was blue.

She let herself fall onto the bed, and images crossed her mind. In this same bed, earlier, he had recounted his past life to her, the tedium of the streets in Ciudad Mendoza, what men and women did there in order not to die of boredom.

Three days later Angelica arrived in Ciudad Mendoza. There are not many tall blonde women in that town. She spotted them, mother and daughter, in the market. To be certain, she passed near enough to them to recognize the streak of white in the mother's hair. "And to think it was on her account!" she shouted to herself. A few steps away she leaned over, and feigning to be interested, inquired the price of a fruit whose name she did not know. She listened: the foreign women were speaking Finnish. Everything bore out what her dead lover had told her.

She followed them through the city, remaining some distance behind them, and was pleased to find them making for the hotel. The three entered the lobby at the same time. She saw them disappear behind a door at the far end. Then she went upstairs to her room and lay down to rest, and to wait.

The sound of children came up from the street below. Angelica went on remembering. It seemed to her that what she was going to do tonight would break into the repetitiousness of her life. She felt close to Manuel. Not once did she think of wrongdoing. When twilight came, she undressed in order to bathe and change her clothes; only then did it occur to her that she would be measuring her strength against the strength of a man. She opened her handbag to take out a ring, which she slipped onto her finger. A certain serenity shone in her eyes.

She went to the dining room and sat down by herself to eat. An inner voice had told her to cease thinking. Things happen; we are only the instrument.

A man came up to the table. Before looking up she was aware of the Italian accent; out of the corner of her eye she saw the wedding ring on his finger. She let him sit down beside her. They talked, and shortly she knew his name. "I never saw him," Manuel had told her. "Cavalcanti. The same name as the hotel."

Angelica drank her coffee and rose from the table. "I'll be seeing you," she said as she walked away. He watched her move off and leave the room; he heard her going upstairs.

Before dying, things are seen in another light; perhaps the eyes know they will not see them again.

At that point Carlo Cavalcanti was listening to the various voices of the night, and to the sound of his own breathing. His wife and daughter looked into the dining room and greeted him in Finnish, before going on. He did not move. He stared into his empty coffee cup and moistened his lips. His footsteps echoed in the lobby. From the dark end of the hall his wife watched, with resignation and hatred, as he started to climb the staircase. He shut his eyes. There was light in the upstairs corridor. He smoothed his eyebrows and knocked. Silently the door opened.

Before he could wonder what had happened, he was lying on his back. From the floor he saw the long barrel of the silenced revolver. He raised his hands to his abdomen: blood, and an impossible stench. Still without understanding, he saw the woman leaning over him. And from within a cloud he was aware of the nimble fingers that loosened his belt and uncovered his sex. A tiny knife brought him out of his stupor. "*Maldita,*" he managed to say, but the sound of his voice convinced him that he was already in hell.

Angelica watched: the dying man's lips were partially open. She forced the point of the knife between his teeth, and pried open his mouth. From the black emptiness welled black blood. At that moment she had a living vision of Manuel as he had lain dead, his sex thrust between his jaws.

Angelica left the town before dawn.

The Host

It is said that in the middle of the island, at the cloud-covered summit of the mountain, there is a lake of great depth, like a blue eye looking up at the sky. And in the center of the lake is another island, a tiny pile of rocks, the abode of a lone man who, perhaps because he has always been by himself, is not really a man.

The man is old now, and does not remember the people who live down on the island. Even on the clearest days, although he climbs to the highest rock, he is unable to see the land surrounding the lake, which he conceives of as infinite. Sometimes in the night he dreams and sees faces and other sights which he fails to understand; then he senses that he is alone and that he ought not to be alone. When he awakens he feels cold, and if there is a wind, from his cave he can hear the ceaseless rise and fall of the water between the rocks.

A flock of goats lives on the little island. They live on the leaves of the fig trees that grow here and there among the rocks. The man, who eats the figs and drinks the milk of the goats, thinks of himself as fortunate; but when he dreams of those faces — and there are arms with the faces, and many eyes staring at him — he becomes like other men: he feels lost, understands nothing, without knowing what it is that he feels and cannot understand. The full moon, the goats which sometimes run away from him, the water which on certain nights sounds particularly clear, the cave itself or the rocks rising against the sky, each could enclose a secret. The man foresees it: the end, the final hour, the boat which brought him as a child to the island, and which will soon arrive to take him away. One day at sunrise he will see a sail, a white spot on the western horizon. Something will be revealed to him that day. The dream of the faces will no longer seem absurd. He will see that which he once saw but has now forgotten, things which he knows only in his dreams. For an instant he will break free of the mystery, only to be enveloped in another mystery.

The moon set; the water, the earth, the sky, and the man watching became one in the darkness. After a long silence, a ray of the sun illumined the sky. The air was so clear that the man, who had climbed to the top of a high rock, could see the spume of the waves as they hit the prow of a boat moving in the distance. The goats gathered around him. One of them came nearer and lightly touched his leg. The man knelt and drank some of its milk. For a moment he managed to efface the image of the boat from his mind, but when it turned (since it was now only a few yards from the shore) the flapping of the sail was audible above the sound of the wind, and both man and goat looked up. The pilot waved a greeting with one hand,

while with the other he grasped the rope governing the boom.
The old man went down to the shore and waited for a wave to
arrive before jumping into the water. He swam to the boat and
climbed aboard. The pilot looked him up and down, and the
old man felt ashamed. He glanced down at himself and felt the
weight of his hair and the long beard which covered his chest.
Another man came up on deck from below, and now the old
man was afraid. This one wore a yellow cloak that shone in the
sunlight. He approached the old man, stretched out his hand,
and removing a twig that had got entangled in his beard,
tossed it into the water. The mouth of the cave was visible
from the boat; the goats had disappeared. The old man looked
down at his hands: the long nails were twisted. The sun shone
in the sky, the surface of the lake was a mirror.

(The veins emptied of blood, the entrails cleaned by the man
in yellow — and relieved of the white snake living in them —
the old man's body, which has been sacrificed on the deck, is
thrown into the water. It is said that the lake is bottomless.
The boat continues its course eastward, and at sunset is
beached on the sand, while songs of praise are chanted by
those watching. The man in yellow, still aboard, raises both
hands aloft, and the snake writhes in the air. Silence. Thirty-
eight boys wait on the beach. Their bodies, seen from above,
foot against foot, hand in hand, form a star. When the moon
rises, the snake is set free; someone leaves it on a disc in the
center of the star. During the night it chooses from among
them its new host, and the next day the boat sets out with
them for the island.)

People of the Head

I met Luisa at the Baby Doll Lounge. The first time I saw her, or that I remember seeing her, I was reminded of Lucrecia, my earliest girl friend, about whom I had long since ceased to think. When she stopped dancing she came and sat by my side. Like me, she was thin, with deep-set eyes. She was my age, but her skin was dry and her forehead was lined with premature wrinkles. She seemed timid. I mentioned this to her, and she replied:

Yes, yes. And I hate this place. But soon everything will be different.

I said I hoped that was the case. I paid for her drink and said goodbye.

The second time was one morning as I was walking to work. She was wearing a black coat and her face was pale. She ran past me. I began to follow her, but she turned a corner and I lost her. That day when I left the office I went back to the Lounge, but without finding her.

I did not enjoy my work. Afternoons, in spite of being tired, rather than go home I would roam the streets until twilight, but it was as though the one walking were not I. If anyone had asked me why I went to the places where I went, I should probably have hit on some pretext. I was like the philosopher's stone which, on being thrown into the air, believes this was its own intention. After a space of three months I paid a visit to the Baby Doll Lounge. It was a rainy night, the last Friday in April.

I no longer drink, but that night I did. A woman was dancing while she watched herself in the mirror. I saw Luisa at the far end of the bar, talking to a man. Soon she was at my side. She drank along with me. I don't remember what she told me, but I was content, and ended up without any money. Then she spoke of Wing Hung Wong. It was he who was watching us from the end of the bar. Luisa took my arm and led me over to him. He was short, and his hand was damp and cold. Luisa spoke into his ear and hugged him. As soon as I could I found a pretext for leaving.

I saw Luisa two days later at a bus stop. She told me she wanted to speak with me, and I suggested she have coffee with me that afternoon when I left work. She seemed eager to convince me that Wing Hung Wong was a good man. He knew a great deal, she claimed, and was a financial genius. He had come from China at the time of the Destruction. He lived in an anonymous old building several stories high. He had liked me, she said, and he wanted to know if there was any way in which he could be of use to me. I laughed, and Luisa must have noticed my skepticism, for she went on: I assure you he doesn't want anything from you.

When we said goodbye I told her I would consider making his acquaintance. They claim that this is precisely what constitutes the immoral act, but there was not much to consider. When I got home I had made up my mind to find out in what way Wing Hung Wong thought he could be of use to me.

The following morning I did not get up to go to work. About ten the telephone rang. It was my superior, and I let the answering service take care of him. I spent half the day by the window, watching the people go by in the street. I arranged the books on the shelves. I opened one volume at random and read: Let us imagine ourselves transported to a very lonely place. Wing Hung Wong telephoned to invite me to dinner.

I told him I was sorry, and went out for a walk. I was a little perplexed.

On my return I found a piece of paper under my door. It was from Luisa, and it surprised me because I had forgotten that I had told her where I lived. Wing Hung Wong wanted very much that I go to his house. My presence would please him; it did not involve me in anything, she said, and she hoped I would go. On the back of the note there was a diagram showing how to find Wing Hung Wong's residence.

At eight o'clock I was at the door. I rang the bell, heard the buzzing of the lock, and pushed. Four steps led up to a landing; the hallway was to the right. In a dim little room there was a chair, an umbrella stand and a mirror. A wide staircase led up to the second floor. I found more light up there. A carpeted corridor took me to a room where there was a low table and a couch. There, standing beside a tall black urn was Wing Hung Wong. We did not shake hands. It was clear that he was surprised. I'm glad that Luisa was able to persuade you, he told me. She would arrive a little late, he continued. He served me tea, and then he left me alone, saying that he would be with me shortly.

In the center of the table was a small ivory statue, representing an elephant being attacked by five tigers. At its base a plaque read: The soul and the senses. I rose and went over to the opposite wall, where on a shelf there were tortoise shells, ancient Chinese coins, yarrow stalks, and wings of black feathers. I approached the urn, and saw that it was decorated with a snake and a heron which were fighting for possession of a fish caught in a silver net. From the mouth of the jar came a rancid odor. I craned my neck and peered inside, then turned quickly toward the door, having heard a voice. Those things require time, Wing Hung Wong was saying. You'll have to wait. Yes, seven weeks. When he came back into the room he said: I've ordered some oysters from the Jade Palace on the corner. They're delicious. I hope Luisa won't be too late.

It seemed a good idea to talk about Luisa; I asked him where he had met her.

Where you met her, he said. A year ago. If you work as hard as I do it's good to amuse yourself now and then.

I agreed. He asked me what I worked at.

Nothing, at present.

Do you have many friends?

I have none.

He coughed, and began to speak about his past.

I slept badly that night. I had eaten many oysters, and Luisa failed to arrive. As I tossed in bed, I said to myself that Wing Hung Wong was a tired and vain man. I'm a statistician, he had said, but people consult me as though I were an oracle.

The following day I went back to work, only to be told that

my services were no longer required. I emptied the drawers in my desk and went home. In the evening I went to look for Luisa at the Baby Doll Lounge. I asked after her from some of the dancers and from the bartender. She should have arrived hours ago, they told me; nobody knew where she could be found. It occurred to me that I might never see her again, and at that moment I remembered what Wing Hung Wong had said to me the night before as we were eating: Girls like that are not important. I decided to go and see him, since he lived not far, in the hope that he might know where I could find her. I rang several times at his door, but there was no answer. So much the better, I thought.

I've always liked the days that go by between one job and another, when it is possible to enjoy idleness, without tasting the artificial flavor that holidays have. Those are the days when you get to know new places and discover new streets because you walk without a definite goal, and return home rich, perhaps with a rare book under your arm, a book for which you paid very little. One of those afternoons when I returned home from a long walk, I stopped to look at some volumes which an old woman had spread out on the sidewalk. Suddenly it began to rain, and the woman gathered up the books, which she packed into a box. When she had finished, she said to me: Wouldn't you like them? I'll let you have them cheap. They're heavy, and I can't carry them all home with me.

I gave her what little money I had on me.

When night came, after going through the books, most of which were valueless, I sat down in the armchair and began to leaf through a battered volume of the *Ghaya al-Hakim*. This was how I first became acquainted with the holy men of Harrán, whom their enemies qualified as 'the people of the head.' Their prestige, based on the infallible predictions they made of future events, rapidly declined when it was learned that in order to make their prophecies, they stood a man in a high urn filled with sesame oil which reached to his chin. Here he was kept for an indefinite period, nourished with figs, until his tissues were saturated with the oil, so that his torturer had only to pull him upward by his hair to separate the head from the trunk. The head then foretold the future.

I was about to write some lines in my diary when I remembered the tortoise shells, the Chinese coins, the yarrow stalks, the black feathers, and Wing Hung Wong's urn. I recalled his words: I'm an oracle to some people. As in a nightmare, I saw Luisa's head between his hands. I shut the book and went out into the street.

At the Baby Doll Lounge they told me that Luisa had been absent for several days. I walked to Wing Hung Wong's, but did not dare to ring at his door. It's not impossible, I thought, but I can't believe it. My ideas were absurd. I laughed, and then felt fear. I went into the Jade Palace, sat down by a window, and ordered a series of dishes that I scarcely touched. The smell of the noodles disgusted me. I called the waiter and asked how they had been prepared.

With sesame oil, he said.

I pushed the plate aside. It smelled like Wing Hung Wong's urn.

It was midnight when I got home. I opened the book and reread the passage on 'the people of the head.' These things need time, Wing Hung Wong had said. Seven weeks. With whom had he been speaking? Day was beginning when I managed to fall asleep.

When I awoke, the preceding evening seemed far away, and my fears struck me as ridiculous. There was nothing extraordinary in the fact that Luisa, a dancer, should have disappeared. Wing Hung Wong was doubtless an eccentric, but that was no reason for thinking him a murderer.

I telephoned various employment agencies in the hope of finding work. I addressed several envelopes and set out for the post office. As I waited in line, it occurred to me to see if Wing Hung Wong's telephone number was in the book. When the letters were stamped, I went over to where the telephone books were piled, attached with chains to metal bars. I found the listing; after the name I read *Financial Predictions.*

I went home and dialed the number. The answering service requested that I leave my name or that of the company I worked for, the purpose of my call, the date, the hour, and the number from which I was calling. I hung up.

It was noon. I tried to collect my thoughts.

Wing Hung Wong, who had made his money giving financial advice, had a collection of objects used in divination, and next to them, an enormous urn which smelt of oil.

Wing Hung Wong, whom Luisa had called erudite, would be aware of the methods used by 'the people of the head,' methods famous for being infallible.

The oracle demanded an urn, sesame oil, and a victim. Wing Hung Wong, who had remarked of Luisa: Girls like that are not important, had such an urn and Luisa, who had assured me that he was a good man, had disappeared.

On the other hand, I thought, Wing Hung Wong had attempted to be friendly with me. Perhaps my suspicions were ill-founded; perhaps Luisa was not in danger, but had been only an instrument, the intended victim being me.

The telephone rang. It was he; his manner was obsequious. He was inviting me to lunch. Before I could reply, I heard the voice of Luisa.

Where have you been? I asked her. I went several times to look for you. Nobody knew where you were, and I began to worry. Are you all right?

I've never felt better, she said; her voice sounded natural. I spent a few days at the beach. I'd been needing a vacation. Wing invited me. Excuse me for not coming the other night. I was terribly tired. Are you coming?

I said I would. From the desk I saw the book of the *Ghaya al-Hakim,* lying open on the small table beside the armchair. A draught riffled the pages. I made an entry in my diary and got ready to go out.

I had walked halfway to Wing Hung Wong's house when I stopped. They're going to put me into the jar, I thought. They would have denatured the food with a soporific, and upon coming to I should have realized what had happened. I would be gagged, perhaps, and there would be a tube in my throat for Wing Hung Wong to feed me through. Luisa knew that I lived alone, and I had told Wing Hung Wong that I had no friends. With a certain sadness I thought of the considerable time that would go by before anyone became aware of my disappearance. Slowly I continued to walk.

Perhaps this was the last time I should see the street: the shop windows I never looked into, the grains of mica in the sidewalk. I should never again breathe this impure air. At the same time, I felt that nothing would happen. Then it was as if, basically, I should have been pleased to see my fears realized. Not that I wanted to be the victim, but I should have liked to prove that I had been able to foresee my destiny.

The door was ajar. I did not ring the bell. I climbed the staircase silently. When I got to the hall I heard Luisa's laugh, and

Wing Hung Wong's voice.

I went into the sitting-room. Luisa seemed healthy and happy, years younger than my memory of her. Wing Hung Wong, who rose to give me his hand, looked harmless. The lunch, provided by the Jade Palace, was served.

As we ate, I found myself discarding the certainties I had been holding, until the odor of sesame brought me up short. The other night, I said to Wing Hung Wong, who was smiling at me, I didn't ask you what all those things were.

I pointed to the objects on the shelf.

Oh, everybody asks about them, he said. They're antiques, left by my ancestors, who foretold the future according to family tradition. They're oracles, if you like, instruments which I've discovered are just as precise as modern ways of predicting the future.

And the urn, I said. It's not an oracle?

I'm not certain. His face colored slightly. He seemed ashamed not to know.

Luisa stood up. It was two o'clock. At three she had to begin her new work, she explained.

When we were alone, I said to Wing Hung Wong, who had sat down again beside me: Then you've never used the urn. It's a relief to know it, but it's also disappointing. A few days ago I learned of the existence of an infallible oracle, which made me think of your urn. But this particular oracle demanded a death. You mustn't be offended if I tell you I imagined that you might use this method. Understand, if that had been the case, you would have had my approval — at least, up to a certain point. How important is one single life if it makes it possible for man to know the future?

I don't follow you, he told me. Please explain.

I described the discovery I had made in the pages of the book, and the suspicions it had aroused in me.

He said: I suppose my color helped you to think I might be capable of such practices.

Perhaps. But one always attributes one's own qualities to others. There's no other way of being.

So, you could do it? he asked me.

I don't know. But I can imagine doing it.

Wing Hung Wong joined his hands. We could make a fortune. An infallible oracle! But have you thought of the victim? And suppose it didn't work?

To try it out, I said, we'd begin with one of those vagabonds that no one would ever miss.

He recoiled, as if I had suddenly become repulsive to him.

Las Lágrimas

I had been for almost a month in Livingston where I had gone to record examples of the funeral chants of the Garífuna. As soon as I arrived, I realized that the undertaking was not going to be an easy one. It involved gaining not only the sympathy but the friendship, even the affection, of the populace.

I was installed in a bungalow about a mile outside the town, in a grove of coconut trees beside the sea. For a few days it seemed like the life free of worries, of which we all dream. This changed, however, when I became aware that the attempts I was making to establish contact with the inhabitants were meeting with no success.

Upon arriving I had hired a black boy named Agustín to wait on me. When, after two weeks, he asked me when I expected to leave, I explained my project, saying I would not quit the town until I had succeeded in realizing it. Immediately

I saw that I had made a mistake: Agustín was staring at me with suspicion. He would lose no time in spreading the news. It made me uncomfortable. I hoped to gain the friendship of the people, and at the same time I was waiting for one of them to die. Without a death there would be no funeral, and without a funeral I should not get any recordings. I began to suspect that a death had indeed occurred since my arrival, and that the fact had been hidden from me. I said as much to Agustín; he told me there would have been drums. I asked him if he thought I might be allowed to watch the wake if there was one. He did not know; then he added that everything was a question of money. Four weeks had gone by, and I began to consider abandoning the project.

One afternoon when I was walking along the beach I saw a woman and a small girl sitting on the trunk of a palm. They were both crying, and did not notice me until I stopped in front of them. The woman was drawn and pale; the child, who evidently was her daughter, ceased to cry when she saw me. I asked the woman what was wrong.

I have no money, she said. And I need work. She dried her tears. I've left my husband because every time he gets drunk he beats me. If he finds me he'll kill me.

What do you know how to do? I asked her.

I can cook, sir. I'm a woman. And I can wash and sweep.

Beside my bungalow there was an unoccupied hut. I told her she could spend the night there, and if it turned out that I liked her cooking, I should hire her.

The next morning, after showing the woman around the kitchen, I went to look for Agustín, to inform him that I should no longer be needing him. But he had gone out at dawn with the fishermen, and my informants said he would not be back until afternoon. I went past the post office: there was no mail. I asked the postal clerk if he knew Julia, my new servant.

Of course I know her, he said. She's well-known. She works at Las Lágrimas. If you want information, they can give it to you there.

Las Lágrimas was a cantina, not far from the beach, at the end of a dirt road. When I went in, I got the impression that the place was empty. There was no one behind the bar, and the windows were shut. I was about to go out again, when from the corner of the room came the sound of liquid being poured into a glass. I looked, and met the smile of a black man. Pointing at a chair, he said: Please sit down.

I went over and sat with him. He was drinking aguardiente with salt and lemon. He got up, staggering, and got me a glass which he filled from his own bottle. The barman was still asleep, he told me. They were good friends. Where was I from? What was I doing there so early?

When I pronounced the name of Julia, his enormous fist hit the table. The bottle rolled to the floor.

Where is she? he demanded, grabbing me by the shirt. She's my wife.

Telling him to let go of me, I picked up the bottle. The temptation was too strong and I could not resist it. I told him where she was, and not to do anything rash. At that point the barman came in. His entry gave me a chance to leave. I hurried back to the bungalow, looking behind me now and then because I had a feeling that I was being followed.

Julia had not yet prepared lunch. I helped her cut the vegetables and saw that she was not used to cooking. In a sense I was pleased to find that she had lied to me. After lunch, instead of taking a siesta, I went out to walk on the beach. The sky was covered by clouds, and it was not hot.

I walked without stopping as far as the sand bar, where the water was brown. A boy going by sold me two abalones, just out of the sea. I crossed the river, and when I saw that I was alone, I stripped and went into the sea. Afterwards I bathed in the river, to wash off the salt. Then I started to walk back. The fishermen's boats, still far out, were on their way in. Below the clouds the sun appeared, and the sea turned gold.

I found the bungalow door open. In the kitchen a pot containing a roast had been upset on the floor; in the puddle of sauce were the footprints of a dog. I went onto the veranda and began to call out. Then I looked into the hut; it was empty. I shut the bungalow door and began to walk toward the town.

On the main street I met the postal clerk.

Julia's dead, he said. They just found her. At last you've got your wake.

I walked along with him.

Where did they find her?

Where? Where do you think? In the bushes.

I asked him to have a beer with me. He said he had to go down to the port to wait for the last boat, which was bringing some packages, so I went on alone.

At Las Lágrimas the windows were shut, the barman was not there, and the black man seemed not to have moved from his seat in the corner. A candle was burning on the table in front of him.

Ah, it's you, he said when he saw me.

I'm sorry. I lifted his bottle and took a swallow.

Listen. The drums, he said.

He was right. Drums were starting to sound.

Just then Agustín came in.

At last I've found you, he said. I tried to interrupt him, but he went on. The musicians are warming up. Aren't you going to the wake?

I turned to him and in a low voice asked him to go and get the storage battery ready.

You're going to the wake? the black man inquired, once Agustín had gone out.

I felt obliged to explain what I hoped to do.

Music! he exclaimed. I'm a great dancer. But I can't dance where I'm going. Don't think I didn't love her, even though she was what she was. Without her I'm nothing. But the man who lets his wife do as she pleases is a woman. She didn't want to work any longer, and that's why I killed her. But I like you. I promise you you'll have another night of music tomorrow. Your health.

I did not see him pull out the pistol; I breathed again when he put the barrel into his mouth. His eyes staring, he pulled the trigger.

In the street I ran into the barman, with two policemen. They did not stop me, and I ran along the beach, back to my house.

While I was getting things together to take to the wake, I thought: No. Tomorrow I'm taking the boat. The man's eyes haunted me. It began to drizzle as I started out. The chapel was filled with people, and the drums resounded. Agustín had the set-up ready, and I began to record.

The coffin was shut; it was a white casket with a carved floral design. An image of San Isidro, lighted by candles, hung on the wall. A stout woman dressed in blue stood beneath the light, with a red missal in her hands. The drums ceased to sound, and the woman started to pray:

La puerta de cielo tán cerrá
meno la de la lágrima

And the faithful answered:

El tá trite cuandoello tán trite.

From the adjoining room, cut off by a curtain, came the
sound of a child weeping. I turned my head, and an absurd
scene followed. The dead woman's little girl came in, and upon
recognizing me rushed over to where I was. She put her arms
around my legs, and when Agustín tried to pull her away, she
began to scream. I told him to leave her, but she continued to
cry. She stopped only when I picked her up. The woman had
shut the missal, and the drums began once more. The child
grew quiet, and finally fell asleep. From time to time she
opened her eyes and smiled.

I had to hold her all night long. The following day, the priest
took me aside to tell me that the little girl was now completely
alone in the world, and to ask me if I did not know someone
who would be willing to take charge of her. He invited me to
have lunch with him. I let myself be persuaded, and agreed to
take charge of her myself.

Through Agustín I learned that the townspeople were
discussing me. Some claimed that I was a good man, and that
the child could not have been more fortunate. There were
others who suspected less praiseworthy motives behind my
kind deed.

Xquic

If the best of all worlds is one in which at a given moment each thing can become the symbol of any other thing, then in this best of worlds the bottomless black hole which is to be found in a pasture on a ranch called El Retiro (in the lower corner of the Petén on the Mexican border) will become, in due course, the symbol of life for certain members of the faculty of New York University. But in our world life allows no substitutes for emptiness; thus it is not the best of all possible worlds.

One morning in June when the cattle grazed in the high green grass outside the fence that surrounded the afore-mentioned hole, two horsemen came slowly into view. The cattle dispersed and the men dismounted, hitching their horses to the fence. The sun rose higher into the sky; they talked,

---

Xquic, pronounced *shkeek*, is a figure in Mayan mythology.

sweated, and did not smile. The fat one, dark-skinned and with gray hair, spoke quickly in a low voice. The other, young, with Indian features, made a sign of agreement with his head once, and then again. They shook hands before getting on their horses. One went off at a trot toward Esperanza, and the other ambled back to the ruined ranch house.

They did not meet again until several months later, far from that place, one evening during the series of lectures to celebrate the passage of a century and a half since the founding of New York University. The public that night had been amazed by the address delivered by a foreign professor, a plump man with dark skin and gray hair. He spoke of an animal of which there was only one in existence, genus and species at the same time. His arguments met with a cool reception; there were, however, those who were inclined to favor them.

A small group remained in the hall when the lecture was over. Clara Graf of the Science Department expressed an enthusiasm for the idea of the 'unique being' which did not seem entirely sincere. She claimed that she herself had once imagined a similar being, although the foreigner's rigid strictures bore no resemblance to her own concepts, in which dreams were connected to the copulation of insects or the nightly emanations of a certain flower.

"Animals are like numbers," she explained to Antonio, a pale man who did not seem to understand. "Like numbers composed of other numbers."

"This being is a key cipher, something like zero or the incommensurable π," said Joaquín, the young man with Indian features.

Antonio turned and recognized Joaquín, whom he had not seen for several years; seeing his face reminded him of his childhood. He shook hands with him and interrupted Clara to introduce him. Meanwhile someone remarked that to categorize the various forms of life according to genus and species was a useless task because each class and each individual is nothing in itself.

"To classify an animal according to the number of its legs would be like using numbers according to the size of the angles and arcs that form them."

"Life is like an enormous tapestry," said an older woman. "If a thread is moved in one place, others are moved in another."

"And Xquic the unique being is the central thread of the warp," said the foreign professor, who had approached silently.

It seems to me that things happened all at once, writes Antonio in his travel notebook, sent to the University from El Retiro, *that each stage along the way bringing me to the place where I am is separated from the next by an impassable obstacle.* It was December. Urged by Clara on the one hand, and by Joaquín on the other, he had undertaken the trip to the place where, according to an article by the stout professor published in the faculty press, "the unique being" had been discovered. *A short while ago I was walking on the campus with Clara, discussing an impossible creature, a "unique being." Now I am writing by the light of an alcohol lamp, surrounded by darkness and the forest.* He speaks of the possibility of believing in the incredible; cites Francisco Sánchez, who four centuries ago wrote that the leaves of certain trees, upon falling into a river in Ireland, became fishes, and that the bear licks her cub to give it a shape.

Antonio had traveled up the Chixoy in a canoe made of the trunk of a ceiba tree, along with twelve people whose faces he could not see, except for a child sitting on his right, whom he looked at over his shoulder, and who from time to time put its hand into the water as if it wanted to change it into a fish.

The river there is narrow. On both banks, outside the forest, there is wire strung along live yucca stalks; farmhouses have roofs of thatched palm. Here a long paddock in the mud, with seven dirty horses standing motionless; there one gray heron surrounded by white ones. The weeds in the undergrowth have long sword-shaped leaves, or round star-like ones. They pass over the framework of a sunken bridge. A tributary pours brown water into the green river. A newly fallen tree causes the water to jump and splash.

He spent the first night in a village: eight or ten dingy houses beside the river, where the boat stopped when the quick dusk fell. The forest air, he says, made him feel heavy, as if from a drug.

His dreams, quickly forgotten, left an unpleasant taste with him. He breakfasted at sunrise in a hut by the river. A deaf-mute child with no tongue came to sit opposite him at his table.

He managed to get me to give him some food, and afterwards some coins. It made me feel better to have given him something. In his tortured sign-language the boy recounted violent occurrences which it seemed he had witnessed: a man stabbed to death, a poisoning, a shipwrecked man devoured by a fish.

Antonio asked the woman who brought the food if she knew where the boy was from. She did not know him; he had appeared the night before on the path running parallel to the river, going in the direction in which Antonio was headed. Antonio found it strange that the child inspired respect in her — perhaps even fear.

He continued the trip in the same dugout, with a different

boatman. The river was narrower, and the trees met overhead, forming a tunnel. Now Antonio sat in the stern of the boat, beside a shirtless man whose body was weather-beaten by the sun. Ahead were two young women, both with long tresses of oily black hair.

They stop at midday to lunch. Antonio complains of the heat, does not eat. He writes: *Clara, the reason for this journey, lives in the midst of books, in a cold climate, like a transplanted flower under glass. She believes in an orderly world in which disorder exists only to give us hope, so as to allow us to doubt. I, sweating and full of loathing for the mosquitoes, can't believe that the world is anything but chaos. I'd like to have undertaken this voyage without any reason, with no object.*

He found the camp in the expected place, at a bend in the river. First he saw the limp flags: the rectangular one of the republic, and the university's triangular one. The camp consisted of a whitewashed hut a few feet from the shore, with four military tents arranged in a semicircle around it. When the boat man shut off the motor Antonio heard the sound of another motor on land which quickly stopped running. A short blonde woman came out of one of the tents. Another appeared in the doorway of the hut, which gave onto the dock over the river. She also was short, but her hair was black and her skin was the color of the people of the region. Antonio got out of the canoe. From the beginning, he writes, there was a misunderstanding.

"Señor Inspector?" she asked him.

The dugout was leaving.

"Tomorrow at ten!" shouted the boatman, removing his hat to say goodbye.

The woman, whose name was Iris, was dressed like those of

the village where Antonio had slept the preceding night. *I let her continue under the mistaken impression,* he explains, *because for some reason I felt like an intruder.* Nevertheless he admits to finding it unflattering that he should have been taken for a government inspector.

Soon he realized that he should not have accepted the error. The woman was not a simple servant as he had assumed when he had first seen her. She spoke Spanish as well as Mam (her native tongue) and on going into the hut Antonio noticed that she had been reading a German magazine.

"If you don't mind," he said, in order to avoid having to make conversation, "I'd like to have a walk around outside."

The pretext was a valid one: after a journey in a dugout one needs to stretch one's legs.

"Of course," she said. Turning toward the door she called: "Ann!"

Ann was the blonde woman he had seen coming out of one of the tents. Iris indicated that Ann should accompany him.

She came running, her cheeks flushed from the exertion.

The two women and Antonio walked toward the center of the camp, where the generator was housed. From there one could see, to the north, a straight path which lost itself among the trees. And to the east was another, winding along beside the river.

"You can go out this way and come back that way," Iris said. "Or vice versa."

Antonio chose the straight path without knowing quite why. Ann was speaking of the research, something about balance and harmony and the interrelation of the species, statements which he had heard from Clara, and which wearied him. He wondered if Ann were not bored living here, but he did not dare ask her, because it seemed to him that it would not have been a proper subject for an inspector to discuss. The path, completely straight, made Antonio think of an aisle in a cathedral.

"How far does it go?" he asked.

"Don't you know?" Ann was surprised. "It's the path to the well of Xquic."

They walked in silence for several minutes.

"What are you thinking about?" Ann murmured when they stopped.

The water in the well was crystalline, he had written on the last page of the notebook, *and the stick Ann handed me to thrust into it did not modify its direction as it penetrated the surface. At the bottom, which was of gray sand, there were three concentric circles. An almost imperceptible motion, slow and regular, made me lean over the water. On the surface I saw my face, my mouth partially open; I moved back. There was a metallic odor in the air.*

In the center of the well, near the bottom, appeared a point which drew the light to it. It did not touch the bottom; it cast a shadow over it in the form of a comma. It seemed to grow from within, to issue from itself, from the transparent water, from nothingness. It turned very slowly upon itself and as it turned it changed, or took on, shape. I experienced a slight dizziness, a coldness on the nape of my neck, a feeling of unreality, as from a blow on the head.

What had taken shape was the fossil of a snail, carefully imperfect, with a crack here, a hole there. It grew until it reached the edge of the well, and disappeared.

The light was fading. Ann had begun to walk towards the camp along the river path. I followed her.

"There's no doubt, Professor," Clara said. "It's his handwriting." The notebook, small and black, was the worse for wear. Clara stood up and let it fall onto the table. Feeling suddenly dizzy, she rested her hand on the back of the chair. "It's farcical," she thought. Antonio, she suspected, had no intention of returning. There was something — she did not know precisely what, about the professor, with his glassy eyes and gray hair which inspired distrust. It was Antonio's handwriting, slightly smaller and more crowded than usual, which could have been due to his desire to save paper. But perhaps there was some other explanation. She turned toward the wide windows: it was night and snow was starting to fall, white, soft.

"The testimony of your friend is of the utmost value to us," the professor told her.

This was true. Antonio was a skeptic. Clara realized the irony: Antonio was credulous and she was beginning to doubt.

"He didn't believe," the professor continued. "But he went where few people have gone and saw for himself. Others believe without having to stir from where they are."

"Like me," said Clara. The image of Antonio following Ann flashed across her mind.

"Like you," agreed the professor, rising to escort her to the door.

The idea of its being a snail has produced results, said the note which the professor sent Joaquín, waiting for news at El Retiro. *The publication of the Science Department has announced the granting of the necessary funds for the continuation of studies regarding the well of Xquic. Best to Antonio. Remember me to Iris and Ann.*

After reading the note Joaquín put on his boots and went out onto the veranda, where the boards were rotten. He gave orders to a youth lying in a hammock to go to Esperanza for ice and beer. He went around the outside of the house and found Antonio lying on his back in the green water of the narrow swimming pool. There was no Iris, no Ann.